MW00990560

Dear Terry

by Joyce Voelker

Poems by Christine M. Voelker

Bob Jones University Press, Greenville, South Carolina 29614

Dear Terry

Edited by Mark Sidwell

Cover designed by Cheryl Weikel; photo by Unusual Films

Photo Credits:
Suzanne R. Altizer: 19
Kathy Pflug: 50
Tourist Division, Georgia Department of Industry and Trade: 39

ISBN 0-89084-526-3

Printed in the United States of America

20   19   18   17   16   15   14   13   12   11   10   9   8   7

Publisher's Note

Joyce, the main character in this story, is a fifth-grader who is blessed with a large family and Christian parents. Although she is a Christian too, she still worries about things such as moving to a new state and making new friends. Of even greater concern to her is the illness and decline of her beloved Granny, who has always been an important influence in her life.

When Joyce found that she didn't like keeping a diary, it was Granny who gave her Terry's name and encouraged her to start writing to a pen pal. Joyce's letters to her pen pal in Vermont chronicle the events of her adventurous life, told from her unique viewpoint. They reflect her opinions, her anxieties, and her triumphs. As she shares her thoughts with Terry and becomes involved with her new friend's problems, she learns to express her faith in Jesus Christ and to trust God for her Granny's future.

143 Grandview Drive
Columbus, Ohio
December 29

Dear Terry,

My grandmother says that I should have a pen pal. She found your name and address in a magazine. So–here I am writing to you. I didn't really know what a pen pal was or why I should have one. Granny (that's what I've called her ever since I can remember) explained that writing letters can be like a hobby–something to do when I get bored. I guess she thinks I get bored a lot.

Anyway, here's how I got started on this thing about being pen pals. One day my schoolteacher (I'm in fifth grade. What grade are you in?) wrote a note home to my parents. It was stapled to a story I had written in class. I knew I wasn't in trouble or anything like that because I got an A+ on the story. (Sorry if that sounds like bragging!) Anyway, she told Mom and Dad that I like to write a lot and that they should encourage me. That night Mom went shopping and she came home with a diary for me.

The diary was pink, my favorite color. It even had a shiny gold key. For a few days I really tried to get used to writing in my diary. I knew my sisters always started out by writing "Dear Diary"–but I also knew that "Diary" wasn't anyone's name and "Dear" sounded kind of mushy to me. I felt funny about the idea of writing things down and then not having anyone read them. Even secrets are meant to be shared with someone, as long as you choose the right person (someone who won't blab!).

My sisters write secrets in their diaries, and then they lock them so I can't read any of the good stuff. What they don't know is that I just happen to know where they hide their keys and even before I found them I figured out that a bobby pin or anything like that can open a diary just as well.

I talked to Granny about the diary one day. I can talk to her about almost anything and she always has good advice for me. I asked her what I should do–should I tell Mom I didn't like it or just keep forcing myself to write in it? Granny helped me to see that I should talk to Mom and tell her how I felt.

It took me a few days to get brave enough to tell Mom that I didn't like writing in the diary. I think it hurt her feelings a little, but she seemed to understand. She said I could rip out the used pages and give the rest of the book to my sister who didn't have one yet. Boy, was I relieved!

A few days later Granny called me after school. She was excited about a new idea she had for me. She came over that night with a box of pretty paper and envelopes and explained that I might like to have a pen pal. That way someone would read what I wrote and I'd even get letters back. It sounded great to me, and Mom and Dad liked the idea too. Like I said before–Granny always has good advice.

Dad gave me some money to buy a whole book of stamps. They should last a long time.

Next time I write I'll tell you more about my sisters. Do you have any brothers or sisters? I sure hope you write back soon. I know this will be more fun than the diary.

> Your New Friend,
> (I Hope)
>
> *Joyce*

P.S. Don't worry! I won't really write my letters when I'm bored. If I'm bored, then my letters may come out boring. I think I'll love writing letters!

507 14th Ave. NW
Montpelier, Vermont
January 11

Dear Joyce,

Hi! Boy, am I glad to finally find a pen pal! I sent my name in to that magazine almost six months ago and you're the first person to write to me. Great!! I love to write letters but lots of kids don't. When I write to my cousins, they hardly ever write back. When I do get a letter from them, I can tell that their parents told them what to say. The letters are very short and VERY dull–just like the little notes grown-ups scribble at the bottom of Christmas or birthday cards.

I'm eleven years old and in fifth grade, just like you. I have curly brown hair and lots of freckles which I HATE! I keep waiting and hoping that I'll grow out of them, but for now I'm stuck with them.

No–I don't have any brothers or sisters. I'm an only (lonely) child. Sometimes I wish there were someone to share a room with and play with more often. Our house has four bedrooms but we only need two of them.

We live in the country. Our closest neighbors live about half a mile up the road and they don't have any kids. They're an old couple in their forties. I don't know them very well, but once in a while I ride my bike to their house and play in the yard with their dog. He's a big, playful German shepherd.

My dream is to have my own dog. I want to get a little puppy so I can watch it grow up and teach it tricks and things. Last time I asked my folks, their answer was "maybe." The way they were grinning, I have a feeling I know what I'll get for my next birthday. Sure hope I'm right.

Well–I have to stop writing because it's time for bed. Tomorrow we're having a spelling bee at school. I really want to win but I doubt if I will. Friday we're going to see my cousins for the weekend. They live about five hours away from here. Can't wait! Hope your weekend is fun too.

Sincerely,

January 18

Dear Terry,

I got your letter yesterday. It sure was fun to get a letter addressed to me. That usually only happens on my birthday or when Mom sends my name in for something free from a cereal box. My birthday is Oct. 15th–when's yours? Every year on my birthday Granny writes me a long letter. That might seem kind of strange since we live in the same town but she writes birthday letters because she says she wants the things she says in them to be for keeps. Last year's letter says I have a laugh like my grandpa's. I love it when Granny tells me things like that. All the letters say she prays for me every day. I read her letters over and over again and they make me feel happy. Granny is special!

It must be different to be the only child. I can't imagine not having to share a bedroom with anyone. I've always wanted a room of my own. It would be nice to be alone when I want to. But you said you wish there were someone for you to play with more often. Mom tells us it's human nature never to be satisfied with the way things are. "The other man's grass is always greener–" or something like that. Granny says, "Be content with such things as ye have." She quotes the Bible a lot.

Sometimes when I want to be alone I go outside and sit on top of the swing set in our back yard. I can't do that in the winter, though. Does it get cold in Vermont? I wish I had a tree house to be alone in, even though that seems like a tomboyish thing to have.

It's never quiet around our house. Someone is always talking, laughing, crying, fighting, or scolding. Guess I'll tell you about my family and then you can decide for yourself if you'd like a bigger family.

My oldest sister is Kathy Ann. She's four years older than me and she's very smart. Seems like I always have the same teachers she had four years ago. They all remind me that Kathy was their BEST student. It doesn't usually take them long to find out that Kathy and I aren't much alike.

I get pretty good grades, but I guess I don't care enough about school to work at getting straight A's like she always does. Mom and Dad are always telling me that I'm not working up to my capabilities–whatever that means. (I had to ask Kathy how to spell it!)

Kathy baby-sits us when Mom and Dad go to parties with their Sunday school class, about once a month. Usually she gets kind of bossy and I get kind of ornery and stubborn. I always end up telling her that she's not my mom and she can't tell me what to do. She would probably have a heart attack if I acted good for a change. It's hard to explain, but sisters can still love each other even though they fight sometimes.

Kathy looks a lot like my mom. She's tall and has dark hair and glasses. Last year they tied for third place in a mother-daughter look-alike contest at our church's mother-daughter banquet. We have a banquet and contest like that every year. Different ladies from the church who don't have daughters or whose daughters live far away usually ask Mom if they can borrow a daughter for the evening. Three of us usually get borrowed and one of us goes to the banquet with Mom. The lady that borrows us buys our ticket and we sit with her for the evening. It's nice that way because otherwise I don't think we'd all be able to go. Mom would go broke buying all the tickets. I always hope my "adopted mom" will sit far away from my real family so I can pretend I'm an only child–just for one night.

Kathy isn't a bad sister. She has lots of good ideas for school projects and I like it when she curls my hair for me.

Donna is next in line. She's two years younger than Kathy and two years older than me. They're so different that you'd never know they are sisters. Donna isn't as smart as Kathy but she does okay and doesn't get in trouble for her grades too often. Actually I never thought it was quite fair how Mom and Dad handle our grades. Kathy and I get a quarter for every A we get on our report cards. Donna and Mary get a quarter for every A or B they get. Mom says that it's perfectly fair because we all have different abilities and God wants us to do our best.

Mostly, Donna is a very kind person. She has a soft heart and she always feels sorry for people who are teased or not liked by other kids. It's easy to talk her into giving me things, but Mom says I shouldn't take advantage of her soft heart. You should see what happens when Donna watches T.V. She laughs so hard at the funny parts, cries her eyes out at the sad parts, and gets up too close to the set when the story gets exciting. She talks to the people on the show as if they can hear her. It's SOOOO funny when she does that!

Donna loves animals–especially horses. She's a fast runner and she can almost always beat me in a race. Donna says she wants to be a ~~vet~~ ~~vetro~~ animal doctor. (I can't spell the longer name for it) when she grows up.

Mary is one year younger than Donna and a year older than me. People call the three of us stair-step sisters because we are each a year apart. Granny says Mom was very busy when we were babies! Mary is closest to my age so we play a lot together. She'll almost always play what I want and lets me be the boss even though I'm younger. We like to play on the swings at the park and talk pig Latin to each other so no one knows what we're saying. Do you know how to speak it?

The worst part about having so many sisters is wearing all the hand-me-downs. Boy, are they worn out by the time they get to me!

Do you and your family go to church? Do they have a mother-daughter banquet at your church?

Well, I've got to stop writing and get busy on my school work. I hope you had a good time at your cousins' house. Write and tell me about it.

Your Friend,

P.S. I'll write about my little brother in another letter–he's seven.
P.P.S. What does <u>P.S.</u> mean anyway? I've always wondered.

January 25

Dear Terry,

You probably just got a letter from me–but guess what? We're moving next month! I just found out today and boy was I surprised. Dad says he got an offer for a better job in Iowa. That's the state where he was born and grew up. The name of the town is Cedar Rapids and we're going to live with his mom until we find a house of our own. I've never met my Grandma Long before. I don't think I will like her as much as my Granny. I'm so upset about moving away from her.

After Dad told us the news I called Granny and begged her to move with us. I was crying and crying but I didn't even care. She told me she couldn't move but that everything would be okay. I DOUBT THAT! How can I ever leave Granny?

Grandpa Long died when I was just a baby. I never met him either. He was sick for many years with tuberculosis (TB for short). TB is a dangerous disease and easy for other people to catch so they had to build a separate building for Grandpa to live in. It was in the yard right next to their house. No one could visit him because they might get the disease too. After Grandpa died they burned down the building. He spent lots of time in the sanitarium–that's like a hospital.

Mom told me that modern medicine and science are wonderful. They have come up with new medicine and shots to keep people from getting diseases like TB and polio. So, even though I hate shots, I guess it's a good thing to get them sometimes.

Anyway, I think moving to Iowa will be scary. Every time I think about it, I miss Granny, and we haven't even left town yet. She told me how much I'll like meeting Dad's side of the family but I know she'll miss me as much as I miss her. I know I'll never be as close to Grandma Long.

Dad has lots of relatives in Iowa so we'll meet aunts, uncles, and cousins we've never met before. I guess I should just trust God and not worry about things I can't change, but it's hard to do that.

Mom says Grandma Long's house is very small so she hopes we don't have to stay there long. I wonder if she bakes cookies and cakes like Granny? Granny's house always smells like vanilla and cinnamon.

Grandma Long wants Dad to build an inside bathroom. Can you believe she still has an outside one now? She sure is way behind the times. I wonder how she takes a bath????

Well, I won't write again until we get moved in. Then I'll tell you all about it. My new address in Iowa is on the envelope.

Write Soon!

Joyce

February 23

Dear Joyce,

ESYAY! I OWKNAY OWHAY OTAY EAKSPAY IGPAY ATINLAY! (YES! I KNOW HOW TO SPEAK PIG LATIN!) Wow! It sure was hard to put it in writing though. Hey! Maybe we could come up with a secret code some time. Then if we write any secrets we won't have to worry about someone finding them out.

My birthday is March 16th. I'll be 12, which is seven months (minus one day) older than you. Sure hope I get a puppy for my birthday. If I do, I'll send you a picture.

Reading about your sisters was fun. But when you talked about being stair-step sisters it sounded like the name of an acrobatic act at the amusement park near here. You know how they say, "And now, ladies and gentlemen–the group you've been waiting to see–the fabulous Stair-Step Sisters! Let's give them a big hand."

I also learned a new word from you. I'd never heard of hand-me-downs. My mom laughed when I asked her about it. She and Dad both came from big families and always had clothes passed down to them from older brothers and sisters. Of course that can't happen in my family since I'm the only child.

A long time ago, I asked Mom why she and Dad never had any more children. She got this sad look on her face and I thought she was gonna cry. Right away I wished I hadn't asked. Later she explained that when I was born she'd

13

almost died. The doctor said she could never live through having another baby.

I wonder if they ever think about adopting another child. Sometimes I want a brother or sister so bad. Either one would be great!

You asked if my family goes to church. Mom goes quite a bit but I usually stay home with my dad. He says Sunday's the only day he can sleep in. Once I went to Sunday school with Mom but I didn't know anyone and I felt kind of dumb. They weren't mean to me or anything like that, but I could tell they were good friends and I felt like I was an outsider.

I get the feeling your family is real religious. Right? I guess you would say my mom is like that but not my dad and me.

No! I can honestly say I've never been to a mother-daughter banquet and I'll probably never go to one. Someday I'll tell you why.

Once I saw a movie on television about a lady who had TB. She had to go live in a sanitarium too. It was sad because she had to leave her family. You're right! We should be thankful for doctors and the ways they've found to keep us from getting diseases like that. It's worth the pain of getting a shot now and then.

Whenever I have to get a shot I turn my head so I won't have to look at anyone. I take a big breath and then hold it and sort of grit my teeth or else I bite on my knuckle. I almost never cry–but my eyes sting.

Well, I hope your move to Iowa goes well. I'm sorry you have to leave your Granny. That'll be hard, but I have a feeling it will all work out for you. In fact, I just know you'll make plenty of friends because you're a very interesting person to know. I'm glad we're friends.

Sincerely,

Terry

P.S. I looked it up and found out that <u>P.S.</u> means "postscript" or something tacked onto the bottom of a letter.

March 18

Dear Joyce,

Since you wrote me two letters in a row, I thought you should get two in a row. I had a wonderful birthday–the best one EVER! YES!! I got my puppy!! We went over to Grandma and Grandpa's like we always do for my birthday. Right away I thought I could hear something whining in the laundry room. I wanted to run in there and check it out but I didn't want to spoil Mom and Dad's surprise so I pretended not to notice. Boy, was that hard!! Grandma even turned up the radio to cover up the noise.

We had lunch and then birthday cake. Then I had to open a present from Grandma and Grandpa–a pair of binoculars which I really like–but I was dying to meet my puppy. It seemed like an hour but it was really only a few minutes after I opened the binoculars when Dad said, "What's that whining noise in the laundry room, Grandpa? Washing machine on the fritz again? Come on, Terry. Let's see if we can help Grandpa fix it."

I tried hard not to grin and not to run in there as fast as I could because everyone was watching me. Mom even had her camera ready to take a snapshot of my surprised face when we opened the laundry room door.

The closer we got, the louder the whining noise, and when we opened the door, my new little fur ball waddled out and ran around in circles. She was so excited that she made a puddle right on the tile floor! Grandma had to go get some rags to clean it up. Mom took a picture of me when I scooped Muffy up in my arms. I chose that name from a book I read. I'd been trying to decide between Muffy or Ribsy (Have you ever read about Henry and Ribsy?) but when I saw how fluffy my little cocker spaniel was, I named her Muffy. Somehow the name fits.

Having a puppy is great. She loves to play with me but Mom won't let her sleep in my room until she's house-trained. Right now Mom thinks that job will take forever. She's sort of stuck with the training because she's home all day while Dad and I go to work and school. I checked out a book from the library about training puppies and told Mom some of the ideas. The book said to take them outside after every nap and every meal. It also said to tie them near their beds because puppies don't like to wet by where they have to sleep. I think Muffy's catching on. I sure hope so because I don't like seeing her tied up or locked in the laundry room.

The first night Muffy was here was awful. Even I wondered if we would keep her or not. She whined ALL NIGHT! I was awake most of the night so my parents could get some sleep. I felt sorry for her but I wanted to go to bed so bad. Good thing the next day was Saturday. Mom let me sleep most of the morning.

The puppy book gave us a good idea about how to make her sleep the next night. You see, she was used to cuddling up against her mother so it said to wrap an old wind-up alarm clock in a couple of soft blankets and let her curl up against it. The ticking noise is supposed to remind her of her mother's heartbeat. That little trick helped for the next few nights and now she doesn't seem to need it anymore.

Thanks for the birthday card and your school picture. I don't have any pictures left and besides, mine turned out awful. My freckles showed up real bad. The only thing that made me feel better when I saw them was that Jimmy (a boy in my class) looked WORSE in his. His mother had cut his hair HERSELF the day before and it looked all chewed up.

Hope I didn't bore you too much with all my puppy talk. Here's a picture of Muffy. I love her more every day!

Your Friend,

Terry

April 30

Dear Terry,

I'm sorry it took me so long to answer your letters. I'll try to explain everything that's happened since we moved to Iowa.

The past few weeks I've missed school because I had scarlet fever. I'm just now feeling well enough to write a letter. I always thought missing school would be fun, but after a while it gets boring. I've spent so much time lying in bed sleeping or staring at the ceiling.

Whenever I was sick in Ohio, Granny would come to visit. She'd always bring a book from the library and read to me for hours. Sometimes I could talk her into telling me stories about when she was a little girl. Like the time she found a baby woodchuck and her mother let her keep it. I love those stories. If only she were here now.

Mom and Dad were sure worried about me when I first got sick. I almost ended up in the hospital. My whole family had to take ~~antie~~ ~~antibi~~ medicine so they wouldn't get sick too. Scarlet fever is very catchy. The doctor's office called a few times to see how I was.

I never knew before that a high fever can make you crazy. It can even cause hallucinations. (How would you like to find that word on your spelling list? Kathy told me how to spell it. Think how rich she'd be if she charged me a dime every time she spelled a word for me.)

I don't understand how using a dictionary can help you find out how to spell a word. How do you know where to look if you can't spell it? And if you do know where to look–that means you already know how to spell it. CONFUSING! That's why I just ask my sister, Kathy–the BRAIN!

Anyway–back to high fevers and craziness. One Sunday night when the rest of the family came home from church I heard them talking in the kitchen. They say I got up and started getting dressed for school but I don't remember it. I do remember being thirsty all the time. Seems like all I did for two weeks was sleep and drink anything they would bring me. I guess I even asked my dad to hook up some kind of a machine over my bed so I could just push a button and get all the drinks I wanted for myself. I don't remember saying anything so dumb!

Mom was right–Grandma Long's house is VERY small for all of us. It smells musty or something, not like Granny's. Grandma sleeps in one room and Mom and Dad sleep in one. The third bedroom is small–even smaller now because Dad built a bathroom in part of it. Mary and I share one bed in this room. It isn't a double bed, so the only way there's room is for one of us to sleep at each end. We've gotten used to it. I don't mind, as long as she keeps her feet clean! They had to put up a cot for her in the living room while I was sick, though. Keith has a bed in Mom and Dad's room.

My other two sisters, Kathy and Donna, sleep on the couch in the living room. They sleep one on each end like Mary and me. If you've ever slept with Donna you'd know you wouldn't want to share a couch or a small bed with her. She's a wild sleeper–kicks and rolls around all night! Mom said we may have to take turns sleeping with her to give Kathy a break.

My great-grandfather, Grandpa Smith, lives close by. He walks up to visit and to eat Mom's cooking lots of times. He's the only Grandpa I've got. I already told you about Grandpa Long dying of TB. Grandpa Hobbes, Granny's husband, died when Mom was only seven–from food poisoning.

Our new school is nice. It hasn't been too bad getting to know the kids in my class. Sometimes the weather is cold for walking to school. I'm trying to get used to it but it really is colder here.

Now that I'm finally feeling better and the fever is down, I sure have lots of homework to catch up on. It's awful!! But I don't want to take fifth grade over again.

The best part of the days now are when Grandpa Smith walks up to visit. He tries to help me with my homework. Mostly he tells me stories and jokes. Here's one for you since you just had a birthday.

''Why are birthdays like false teeth? Because if you keep your mouth shut–no one knows you have them!''

I couldn't believe you didn't know what hand-me-downs are and had to ask your mom. It must be nice to get new clothes. Mine are almost always passed down from sisters, cousins, or church friends.

Well–soon I'll be going back to school but it will be over for the summer in a few months. I wonder where I'll go to school next year? I sure would hate to change schools again just when I'm starting to make friends here.

I guess you could say that my family's religious but I never thought about it that way before. We've just always gone to church all the time. I can't imagine life without reading the Bible together after supper every night. Sometimes I complain about it but deep in my heart I know it's the way a family should be.

Your puppy sounds adorable! The picture is cute! I'm not sure I could make myself stay up all night listening to her whine so I'm glad she's doing better. I like the name ''Muffy''–it seems to fit her just right!

Aunt Nan wrote and said that Granny hasn't been well. They're worried about her mind. Sometimes she can't remember the most simple things. She wasn't like that before we moved. I guess it happened all of a sudden. I'm so worried about her. What if she doesn't remember me next time I see her? I love her so much. I wish I were there to read to her.

Yours Truly,

Joyce

May 10

Dear Terry,

I know it's not my turn to write, but I just felt like writing. I haven't heard about Granny or how she's feeling. I hope that means everything is okay. I wrote her, but she hasn't answered.

I'd give anything right now just to have my own bed! I've given up hoping for my own room! Maybe we could trade families for the summer. Have you ever heard the story about the Prince and the Pauper? That's one of my favorites. But–you're not a rich princess and I'm not really a pauper. I'm not even sure what a pauper is but I think it means a real poor person.

Mom and Dad found a house for us to buy. It isn't real far away, but it is in a different school district. I was afraid that might happen. We'll ride a bus to school because it's outside of town and kids would have to walk along a highway to get there. I guess that wouldn't be safe.

The name of the new school is Prairie Elementary. Then there's Prairie Junior High and Prairie High School. I guess they named them that way because they're out of town–kind of on the prairie. The people from the southwest corner of Cedar Rapids go to school there and so do kids from lots of small farm towns close by. I've already heard the older kids at my church call the school ''Cow Pie High.'' They make fun of it because it's a country school with cornfields and farms all around. The buildings are all pretty new though.

Our new house has three bedrooms. Mom and Dad will have one, Keith will have one to himself (because he's the only boy) and the four of us girls will share one big bedroom. We're gonna buy bunk beds so the room won't be so crowded. Mary and I are the youngest and the lightest, so we'll each have a top bunk.

The house has a big back yard and Dad wants to put a fence around it. There are lots of other houses close by so Mom says we'll have plenty of neighbor kids to play with. We're gonna move in about three weeks.

The funny thing about our new address is the name of the street. We'll live at 5730 Ohio Street. I wrote a letter to my aunt, teasing her that we're moving back to Ohio again.

I sure do like being pen pals. It's easy writing and telling you everything I think and feel. I love getting your letters too. You're special! Someday I hope we can meet each other. I'm busy imagining and trying to come up with a plan to do just that.

Your Pen Pal,

Guess Who?

May 16

Dear Joyce,

Hi! I sure was sad to hear about how sick you were. Glad you're feeling better and hope you are back to school by the time you get this letter.

Things here are fine. Muffy is finally house trained and she's allowed to sleep in my bed with me. Sometimes she crowds me too much, so I put her on the floor–but then she usually sneaks into bed again after I fall asleep.

Mom and Dad are fed up with Muffy because she gets into trash and chews things up. So far she's chewed up two of Mom's shoes (not from the same pair), one of Dad's slippers, and lots of Kleenexes she finds in the wastebaskets. I've caught her chewing on my bedspread a few times too, and on an old sock she found under my bed, but I didn't tell them about that.

The past few days Mom's been sick. Dad and I have been helping to keep the house clean (which isn't easy with a puppy like Muffy around chewing things up–the chewed-up sock makes a good dust rag though!) and cooking for ourselves. Dad's a good cook but he doesn't really like it much. Yesterday I was trying to help him out but neither of us was enjoying it much until we decided to have some fun. We put food coloring in the gravy–a few drops of each color. By the time we were finished, the gravy was purple. We sure did laugh when Mom took a long hard look at it on top of her mashed potatoes.

DEAR TERRY

I guess I kind of understand how you feel about your Granny because I worry lots about my mom too. She seems to get sick easier and more often than most people. You know, I hate to admit it but when Mom was so sick two days ago I was really scared. I kept thinking about how empty the house would seem if she died and it was just Dad and me. I don't like to talk about death because no one really knows what happens next. Does your religion help you understand things like that?

My mom gave me a Bible two years ago for my birthday. I started thinking about how I've never really wanted to read it. But I think I might now.

Anyway, I think Mom's feeling a little better today. I sure hope so. I don't like tiptoeing around and trying to stay out of her way. I've been taking my drawing pad out on the porch or down to my favorite drawing spot. There's a pond behind our house near the woods. Right by the pond is a big oak tree. I love to sit there and lean against that big oak and draw. Sometimes I just sit there and daydream about what I'd like to be when I grow up. I think I may want to be a vet like your sister Donna. I've written some of your letters from the old oak tree too.

Yesterday Dad said he and I will go on a fishing trip after Mom is feeling better. I don't really like to fish but I will go because Dad is just fun to be with. Have you ever been fishing? Do you touch the worms?

Friends,

Terry

May 22

Dear Terry,

I sure was sorry to hear your mom was so sick. I hope she's better now. My family has been praying for her during family devotions. I feel like I understand what you are going through because of Granny getting sick. Aunt Nan wrote that Granny refuses to go to the doctor. Her memory is getting worse and she gets confused easily. Some days she spends all her time in bed asleep.

Your question really made me stop and do some thinking. Remember–you asked if my religion helped me understand and accept death? I feel bad that I haven't told you before what I believe.

You see–I accepted Christ as my Saviour several years ago. That means that I believed He died for my sins and I asked Him to come into my heart. Because of that I know I'm going to heaven when I die. I don't have to be afraid of death because I know what comes next! Your letter made me realize that I really shouldn't worry so much about Granny. She is saved too, so if she does die she'll have a better life in heaven than she has here.

Last Sunday in church I really listened to what Pastor was saying and I realized that faith in God is not a one-time thing. It was exciting and important for me to put my faith in God to save me but it can't stop there. I need to trust God every day with my problems and worries. I made a decision that afternoon to spend time reading my Bible every day and talking to God in prayer. I asked God to help me stop worrying so much about Granny. He knows what's best for her and for us.

Maybe this doesn't make sense to you but I'm not sure I can explain it any better. Please write me back soon. I want to know what you are thinking. We'll keep praying for your mom.

Love,

Joyce

June 5

Dear Joyce,

I got your letter. I didn't answer right away because I didn't know what to say. My mom has talked some about getting saved. Is that the same thing as accepting Christ? I guess I never listened very closely before. I always thought that if it was really as important as Mom said, then Dad would believe it too.

Lately I've been thinking about going to church with Mom once in a while. The way Dad was talking the other day, I think he may even be going. I found out that when Mom was sick the doctor told Dad she would have died if they hadn't caught the pneumonia so early. Dad said something about this being the second time he'd almost lost her and I've noticed he's acting different lately. He's been more thoughtful and serious, like maybe he's thinking about something important. I'm not sure why, but somehow I have a feeling he's thinking about God too.

So—when are you moving? Are you nervous? I've never moved before. We've lived in the same house all my life.

Oh—I have some BIG news to tell you. We got a horse from a farmer who lives close by! It's really a pony, which is more my size, but she's a beauty! She's kind of a tan color with a white mane and tail—I'll call her Blondie. Her coat is so smooth and silky, and I just love brushing her. It's almost too good to be true!! First a puppy of my own— and now a pony! (I'm not sure Muffy is too thrilled about the horse.) Mom told me the farmer just had too many horses and couldn't afford to feed them all so he practically gave this one to us. WOW! I never dreamed I'd have my own horse. What would your sister Donna think? Dad and Mom both know how to ride so they'll teach me.

What do you think about when you're lying in bed at night? Sometimes I make up little poems or stories. I never write them out but I think them out in my head. The other night I was thinking about ''tomorrow'' and it got so confusing. You know, there really is no such day as tomorrow because by the time it comes it isn't tomorrow anymore–it's today. Right?

Did I tell you Muffy chewed two holes in our gold recliner–one in each arm? Then she started pulling out the white stuffing and chasing it around the living room. Dad was furious! Mom stitched it up but you can still see it.

Time for bed!
Your Pen Pal,

Terry

June 15

Dear Terry,

Hurray! School's out for the summer. And we got all moved into the new house. It's so much roomier than living at Grandma's. I love everything about it! The new neighborhood is great.

Dad brought a big tractor tire home from work yesterday and he plans to fill it with sand to play in. If he can get another tire he says he'll fill it with cement and make us a tether ball pole. That should be fun. The swing set is up too, so we have plenty to do when neighbor kids start coming over.

Our new fence is up and the patio is finished too. Having the patio screened in is nice because we can play on it even if it's raining outside. Believe me, it's been raining a lot. On the rainy days when we couldn't play out much, we had fun putting on two puppet shows.

Last night I spent the night at a girlfriend's house. She's the oldest of seven children and her family goes to our church. They live out in the country and they have horses on their farm. Her name is Theresa but she doesn't like nicknames. Theresa's two years older than me.

Well—we got to go riding this morning. She gave me a gentle horse since I hadn't ridden before. I couldn't make the lazy horse move at all. Finally we started moving along sl-o-o-o-wly. Then we came to a bridge over a small stream and for some crazy reason my horse decided to take off running. That took me by surprise since she (or he–I couldn't tell) had been so slow for the rest of the ride. I lost my balance and fell off, but I didn't get hurt–just sort of slid off and landed on my feet, but I was scared to get back on again so we walked the horses back to the barn. Hope your riding lessons are going better than that.

After riding, it was time for lunch. You can imagine what it was like with all seven kids around the table plus me. Theresa's youngest brother is only about one and he was so cute. We were eating chicken noodle soup and while no one was paying attention to him, he grabbed his little bowl and dumped it all over the top of his head. He just sat there giggling with noodles and soup dripping down his face. We all laughed so hard. What a mess!! I sure wish I had a picture of that one.

Later that day we walked down the street to where another friend from church lives and we played there for a while. It was a fun time. I came home about three o'clock this afternoon.

We want to practice a play but we can't agree on which one of the girls has to be the prince. I think Kathy is finally starting to give in a little. She'll make a good prince because she's the tallest and she can make her voice sound almost like a man's. She says it hurts her throat, though. It's so much fun to practice these shows, and then we make invitations for the neighbor kids. Sometimes Mom and Dad even watch us.

Another thing we did was set up a rock museum on the patio. We've been collecting rocks all spring and wanted to do something with them. I got a couple of books about rocks from the library and we found out the names of almost all the rocks we had. We glued them to cardboard, labeled them, and set them up on TV trays. We had a lot of fun even though no one really wanted to come see a bunch of rocks. Mary and I set up a Kool-Aid stand outside the museum. We didn't get rich but we made a few dollars and met a few more neighbor kids. We want to use the money to buy candy from the neighborhood store. I'll tell you more about that in my next letter.

What do you plan to do this summer? Will your family take a vacation? We're going on the first real vacation we've ever had. Some friends of Dad's are loaning us a fold-down camper. All five of us kids, Mom, Dad, and our two dogs are taking a camping trip out to Colorado. I can hardly wait!! Then in August I'll go to a week of church camp. Do you ever get to go to camp? What about this summer?

Write and tell me all about summer in Vermont. Can you send me a picture of you riding your new horse? I bet you ride better than me!

Friends Forever,

Joyce

June 29

Dear Joyce,

Hey–have your ever noticed that your name sounds like "rejoice"? RE-JOYCE! Ha ha. Reminds me of a song I heard in Sunday school last week–something about rejoicing in the Lord always.

All three of us went to church together. Once, during the sermon I looked at Dad's face and I noticed he had that look again–like he was really listening and thinking seriously about something. We've gone to church with Mom before but Dad always seemed bored–like he was only there as a favor to Mom and he'd rather be home in bed. Not this time though. We even went back with her for night church. We've NEVER done that before. Well–once we went on a Sunday night to see her get baptized, but that was different because we hadn't been there in the morning that week.

If Dad is gonna take this church stuff seriously I guess I'd better start listening too. I didn't listen much last week. Maybe I was sleepy from the fishing trip on Saturday. I did like Sunday school better this time. I don't think any of the kids remembered me from before. It was a long time ago. But they were friendly and even shared their Bibles with me. The verses didn't make much sense to me when we read them but the teacher was good and I could understand her just fine. I've got a feeling we'll be going back. Enough about church.

Now about the fishing trip. We left at 6:00 in the morning, which was really early for a Saturday. It took us two hours to get to the lake so I slept a little in the car. Remember how I told you I don't like to fish? Well, it was better this time because we got to ride to the middle of the lake and fish from a boat. We must have sat there for hours before I finally felt something nibbling at my bait. Dad still hadn't caught anything so I was feeling sorta proud. Well–that one got away so I had to put another worm on my hook. I hate those smelly things no matter what anyone says. Don't you just hate it in the spring after it rains and there are all sorts of worms lying around all over the streets and sidewalks? What a smell!

By now we were fishing closer to shore. Anyway, when I cast out the line it went up over a tree limb and then down into the water. I tried to pull it free, but it kinda stuck so I decided to leave it. I wasn't having any luck catching anything anyway so I didn't really care. You'll never believe what happened! Five minutes later while I was daydreaming and sorta making up a poem in my head, my bobber started ducking under the water. I figured I'd snagged some weeds again but it was a bass and this time it didn't get away. I'm probably the first kid to catch a fish out of a tree! It weighed five pounds. Here's a picture of Dad holding the fish.

All for now!

Terry

P.S. Your rock museum sounds like fun. I like to collect rocks too.

July 8

Dear Terry,

I'm so tired today. I didn't get much sleep last night. Let me tell you why.

In the afternoon we decided to try to make a tent to play in. We worked on it a long time, draping blankets over lawn chairs and then over the picnic table. We even tried making it over the clothesline but it kept sagging in the middle. The thing that finally worked was making it over the swing set. We used every old blanket that Mom and the two neighbors could come up with, and it finally turned out okay. Then we started asking Mom if we could sleep out in it overnight. Mom wasn't sure she wanted us to. I think I know why.

Last summer we camped out in a tent in Granny's back yard with our cousins. It was fun, but somehow or other we woke up really early–just as the sun started to come up. We got a little carried away throwing our pillows up in the air and yelling, "I CAUGHT THE SUN! I CAUGHT THE SUN!" Pretty soon we found out it was only five-thirty and we'd woke up everyone. Dad wasn't exactly pleased when he came out to talk to us. Mom was even less thrilled than Dad, but Granny and Aunt Nan didn't say much. I think they were trying hard not to laugh because of Mom and Dad being upset about it all.

Well, Mom finally told us we could sleep outside if we promised not to wake her or the neighbors this time. Of course then my brother got all upset because we didn't invite any boys to stay with us. He and another boy made themselves a little tent too. I think they should have had to wait for another night to sleep out but I decided I'd better not complain.

Mary and I were sent to the neighborhood store to buy candy with our Kool-Aid stand money while the other girls made some popcorn and Kool-Aid to share in the tent. We'd never been there by ourselves and we didn't realize how far away it was. We were on our bikes and we kept thinking we'd gone far enough, but we couldn't find the store. We knew it was in the garage behind a gray house with white trim. Every time we passed a gray house we would ride around and look out back but we never did find the right place.

Later, Kathy went with me and she found the store. She thought she was pretty smart and made me feel like a little kid, but I'm glad we got the candy. They have all kinds of penny candy and gum, so we came back with a whole bag full. On the way home I was trying to show off and ride without holding on to the handlebars. I did okay for awhile but then I skidded in some sand and fell on the cement. OUCH! I tried so hard not to cry but my knees were bleeding and it hurt lots. I finally started crying. Kathy was all embarrassed to be with me and told me I was acting like a baby but I didn't care. For some reason I kept thinking about the time when I was five and we lived in Ohio. Some bigger kid accidentally rode over me on a bicycle. That was even worse than this time, so it cheered me up a little. I sure do hate it when Kathy acts like she is SOOOO grown up and I'm so young. One other time when I was five, I swallowed some little pieces of gravel on the playground. I was afraid and asked her if rocks would grow in my stomach. I thought she knew everything and she knew I thought that. Anyway, she told me that the rocks might grow, so I was afraid about that for the rest of kindergarten and all of first grade. Finally I found out she was just teasing me. I was so relieved that I don't remember getting mad about it.

The camp out was fun but we didn't sleep much. We told jokes and stories and giggled for hours. After that everyone got kind of serious and we started singing songs about Jesus and talking about God. Our neighbors got real quiet. They don't go to church at all. They said they wished they knew more about God like we did. I wish their parents would let them visit our church.

What do you do every day in the summer? Do you get lonely? My sisters and I fight sometimes, but I'd be bored and lost without them to play with!

Aunt Nan wrote to Mom again and said Granny is getting worse. They finally talked her into going to the doctor but he's not sure what's wrong with her. I'm afraid that I may never see her again. But reading my Bible has helped me to trust God more with my fears. I underlined something in my Bible the day the letter came. Here it is: "Trust in the Lord with all thine heart; and lean not unto thine own understanding. In all thy ways acknowledge him, and he shall direct thy paths." (That's Proverbs 3:5-6.) I like those verses. I need to trust Him even when I don't understand why He lets things happen the way they do.

Write Back!

Joyce

July 13

Dear Joyce,

I can't believe all the funny and crazy things that happen to you and your family–like your trip to the store and the rocks you thought would grow inside you.

Your camp out sounded like fun. You know, I sometimes feel like your neighbors did. Remember you said they got real quiet when you started singing and talking about God? I want to learn more about God too. We've all been going to church and I'm learning more but when I read your letters it seems like your family knows God in a different way. It's like He's a personal friend of yours–even a closer friend than you and I are. I hope I get to know Him like that someday.

I've been riding Blondie lots lately and I'm getting pretty good at it. Sometimes I ride bareback because the saddle doesn't fit right. Feeding her and keeping her clean and combed are my jobs now too, but I don't mind at all. I just wish she and Muffy got along better. I think Muffy is jealous of the time I spend with Blondie. I have to leave Muffy in the house when I go riding because her barking drives me crazy.

The other day I did something stupid but it was FUN! Dad was out working in the garage and Mom was at a neighbor's house, visiting. For some dumb reason I started wondering if Blondie would fit through the door to the house. The more I thought about it, the more I wanted to find out for myself. So–I propped the door open and rode her right into the kitchen. What a scene!! Muffy barked and growled and barked some more. Pretty soon she was yelping so loud that Dad heard her and came running from the garage. He thought I was hurt or something. You should have seen his face when he ran through the back door and saw me sitting on Blondie right by the kitchen sink! He was too shocked to say or do anything at first. I didn't know if I was going to get in trouble or not. Then after a few seconds of silence, he burst out laughing, which made me feel a little relieved. I guess he understood my curiosity. Just as I was about to ask him if we had to tell Mom, the phone rang. I was right beside it so I picked it up and said, "Hello." It was MOM!

"Hi! What are you doing?" Mom asked.

I couldn't help it–I burst out laughing even louder than Dad had just done. Then I handed the phone to Dad. He was still laughing too so we had to tell her what was going on. I don't know what Mom said about it all but I'm pretty sure she wasn't laughing like we were. Dad kind of settled down after that. After he hung up he winked at me and led Blondie outside. When I finished feeding her and grooming her I found Dad in the house doing the lunch dishes. Guess he wanted to smooth things over with Mom. Not many mothers want to have a horse in the house, I guess.

Have fun on your vacation. We're not taking one this year. It may have something to do with all Mom's doctor bills but I'm not sure. Send me a post card from Colorado if you can.

Your Friend,

Terry

July 27

Dear Terry,

Our vacation to Colorado was GREAT, even though I didn't get to fly there or stay in motels like I've always dreamed about doing. The car seemed crowded. We were always glad to be done with traveling each day and we were ready to set up camp for the night. Most of the places we camped had playgrounds or else trails for taking nature hikes. It was great!

I couldn't believe there was still snow up in the mountains in July. WOW! But the most exciting thing was coasting downhill for twenty miles of winding roads. The gas gauge said EMPTY and Dad was afraid we would run out of gas and get stranded. If our car had stopped on one of those roads we could have been in an accident, because there is no room for anyone to pass without driving over the side of a cliff. Dad managed to make it all the way down, and then the car stopped just two blocks from a gas station. He had to walk to get some gas but at least we were on level ground.

Kathy wasn't much fun on the trip because she kept getting car sick. Mom gave her some pills that helped some, but we always had to let her sit by the window.

My brother did something really funny last week. At least our family thought it was funny. His Sunday school teacher is very old and her skin is all wrinkled. I guess Keith must have noticed because this is what he said (the teacher told Mom after class).

KEITH: "Teacher–you're old aren't you?"

TEACHER: "What makes you say that, Keith?"

KEITH: "Because your skin doesn't fit you anymore."

Of course Mom was really embarrassed when she heard about it. You really are missing out without a younger sister or brother. They say the funniest things sometimes. It's nice not to be the baby of the family anymore.

I'm glad you want to learn more about God. I really wish you could come to Bible camp here in Iowa. Wouldn't that be great? I don't know how you would get here but imagine what fun it would be to meet each other and stay in the same cabin. Bible camp is the best place to learn about God and the Bible. I guess that deciding to accept Jesus is the most important decision I've ever made. I asked Mom to pray with me that you'll do that too, someday soon.

Love in Christ,

August 2

Dear Joyce,

I really laughed when I read about what your brother said to his Sunday school teacher. I read that part to Mom and Dad and they said I used to say things like that when I was younger too. Mom started telling me some of the things I used to say when I was three. Once when I was trying to tell her my hands were too full of things to carry, I said: "Mommy–I have heavy hands!" I guess I also used to use a made-up word: "amn't." Here's how it would go in a sentence. "I'm growing taller, amn't I?" If I ever get married I sure hope I have a big family like yours, or at least more than one child. Your family seems to always have fun. I love reading about it. Maybe I will save all your letters and I'll write a book someday.

I've been thinking about having a friend over for a camp out. We could set up my pup tent in the back yard. Of course my camp out would only be two people–not at all like yours. I don't invite friends over very often and I'm not sure why. Maybe I'm more of a loner than you. My hobbies all seem to be quiet things to do, like writing poems, collecting stamps, drawing, riding my horse, and reading mysteries.

Do you like to read? I've read lots of Hardy Boy mysteries. I like pretending to be a detective and seeing if I can figure out the mystery before the book tells me what happened.

My uncle John is in the army and he sends me stamps from all over the world. He's been stationed in lots of different countries. He bought me my first stamp album and got me interested in collecting stamps.

No more right now. I've got to take Muffy out to get some exercise, then I'll go for a horseback ride later this afternoon. Lately I've been riding down to the pond and taking a swim. The weather has been beautiful for it. Here's a picture of Blondie I meant to send you before.

Write Back!

Terry

August 7

Dear Terry,

Now that we have a bigger kitchen and more room in our house, Mom has been having company a lot more often. I like it but there are so many rules to remember. Dad and Mom get very picky about table manners when we have visitors, especially if the visitors are grown-ups. If one of us kids is just having friends over it's no big deal. In fact–it's great! We get to pick what we want Mom to fix for supper. I almost always choose hamburgers and French fries with pork and beans. I don't like the beans baked though. Cold ones are my favorites. Wouldn't it be fun if you could spend the night? How about tomorrow? Ha ha!

Anyway–back to telling you about company. This is how things go at our house. First Mom sets the table different. We each have two separate glasses, one for ice water and one for milk or iced tea. Sometimes we even have two forks. One is supposed to be a salad fork but I can never remember which one is which. There is also a separate little plate or dish to put Jell-O salad on so it won't melt and run into the other food. At the end of the meal dessert is served on another clean plate. All of this makes for lots of extra dishes!

Mom always cooks the same things for company dinners and Sunday dinners–roast beef, mashed potatoes, a vegetable, Jell-O, and dinner rolls. I never get tired of the food at company meals. YUM! For dessert she usually makes lemon pie or a pineapple dessert that I love.

The other night Mom was worried that there wasn't enough meat so she found each of us before dinner and whispered to us not to take much. It was hard to pretend I didn't want more. I love roast beef.

After dinner two of us girls have to do all the dishes. One person washes dishes and cleans off the table. The other person dries dishes and sweeps the floor. We do it the same way on Sundays. Once I was in a hurry and I dried a whole handful of silverware at once instead of drying each individual piece. Dad caught me and very calmly emptied the whole silverware drawer into the rinse water. I had to dry it all piece by piece. Another time he got a plate out of the cupboard and water dripped on his head. I hadn't dried the dishes right so I got to wash and dry the whole set that time too. Believe me, I thought he was mean at the time but I sure did learn my lesson.

What's your favorite food? Are you allowed to drink soda pop very often? We hardly ever get any but we did drink a lot of pop on vacation. It was a great treat. Sometimes on Sunday nights we have a feeling Dad may be planning to give us pop before bed. So we get ready for bed without arguing. Then we climb into bed and strain our ears to listen for the refrigerator door and then the sound of him opening the pop bottles. Half a glass is all we are allowed to have.

Another favorite after-church snack is stopping at the Dairy Queen. I still remember doing that one time when Keith was only three. He grabbed my cone and accidentally smashed it all over his face. All he really wanted was a lick because I had already been sharing with him. I was upset because he ruined my ice cream cone but he was such a mess I had to laugh with everyone else. He was screaming because it felt so cold.

I can't wait until I'm a grown-up and can decide when I want a snack. Sometimes after Mom and Dad think we are asleep I hear or smell them making popcorn. It just doesn't seem fair.

I haven't told you about Granny yet. It's hard to tell you without the tears coming. Remember how I said she was forgetting things and her mind was going? Well, the other day Aunt Nan called Mom and told her that a neighbor found Granny half a mile down the road. She had put on four or five layers of sweaters and jackets and took off walking without anyone knowing. When the neighbors recognized her they called Aunt Nan. Granny said she was going home. They think she might have thought she was going to walk to the house she grew up in.

The doctors say there is nothing they can do about her mind. Aunt Nan and Aunt Barbara and Uncle Al are going to try to take turns taking care of her. They'll hire a nurse when one of them can't be with her. She can't be left alone anymore. But the worst news was that when Aunt Nan came home from work the other day, Granny said, ''Who are you? Get out of my house!'' A while later she knew her again, though, and didn't seem to remember what she'd said. I'm afraid for Granny! But God is helping me turn my fears over to Him. I did cry about it last night but then I remembered my special verses about trusting and said them over and over.

Your Friend,

Joyce

August 9

Hi again, Terry!

I wasn't planning to write a letter to you today but I just had to tell you about something funny that happened at our house. We were finished with supper and having family devotions around the dinner table like we always do. While Dad was praying, the telephone rang. Donna was sitting right next to the phone but she knew she shouldn't answer it until after the prayer. She reached her hand up and waited until Dad said, "Amen." Then she picked up the phone but instead of saying "Hello" she said, "Our Dear Heavenly Father—"

We were all shocked and Donna got real flustered and embarrassed. One second she was laughing and the next second she was trying to apologize but she couldn't seem to say anything that made sense. Finally the person on the other end hung up. They probably thought they had called the funny farm! It was so funny and we all laughed so hard! We'll probably tease her about it for weeks—maybe even months! I wonder who was on the other end??

Friends Forever,

Joyce

August 14

Dear Joyce,

I was sorry to hear that your Granny is getting worse. Wish I knew how to pray so I could pray for her like you prayed for my mom. I did ask Mom to pray for her. Hope it helps.

I found out yesterday that we do get to take a little bit of a vacation. Really it's just a long weekend trip. We'll leave this Friday morning and come home late Monday night. We're going to a family reunion for Mom's side of the family. I haven't seen them all together since I was a little kid.

Mom had four older sisters but one sister, Pat, died of polio when she was young (in her teens, I think). She was sick a long time. There was a polio epidemic back then. On the day of Pat's funeral, my Aunt Judy started feeling sick and later they found out she had polio too. That must have been hard for her parents–wondering if they'd lose another daughter. She was in and out of the hospital a lot but she didn't die because they caught it earlier. Now Aunt Judy is in a wheelchair from the polio. When she's not in the wheel-chair she has to wear braces on her legs and use crutches. The wheelchair is much easier to use. Her legs will never again work like yours and mine. She even has to have a car made with special hand brakes.

Some kids are scared of people in wheelchairs but if they only knew my Aunt Judy they wouldn't be! She's so much fun. She loves to tease and make jokes. Aunt Judy even has this special, funny voice she uses sometimes. I can't exactly describe it but it's almost like she whistles through her teeth between each word.

Aunt Judy has a nickname for me. (She calls it a "love name.") She's the only person in the world who's allowed to call me "Dimples."

Aunt Judy works in a clinic for handicapped children. As you can tell, she loves kids and understands what these kids are going through. I think anyone is lucky to know her.

My Aunt Jo and Uncle Ed and their kids will probably drive down for the reunion too. Should be the best weekend of my summer. I won't even mind the five-hour drive.

I'm sending along a poem I wrote this summer, and I hope you like it. I've never shown anyone else my poems except Dad and Mom. You're a special friend so I feel safe showing it to you.

Terry

COLORS

Purple, red, white, and blue
Yellow, orange are just for you.
Bright and beautiful–
Dark and dull–
Colors, colors
I love them all!

August 19

Dear Joyce,

You're probably at camp tonight and I'm camping out in my back yard. My friend got the chicken pox and couldn't come so I just set up my pup tent anyway. Muffy and I are sleeping out in it tonight. (Blondie kept hogging all the blankets so we kicked her out–not really!)

I like sitting here with the tent flaps open looking at the stars. I never realized how many bird and animal noises there are at night. I can even hear the cars on the highway about a mile or two from here.

Last weekend was fun. It was fun being with my cousins and other relatives. One thing I really hate, though, is hearing all the grown-ups say how much I've grown (over and over again) or how tall I'm getting. Then they always say, "But you've still got your freckles, don't you?" YUK! But since I don't see them too often I can put up with it. I do love them and I know they aren't trying to get on my nerves. It just happens that way sometimes.

I can't wait to hear about Bible camp. The first time you ever wrote about it I wasn't interested at all. But now, since I've been going to church more, it sounds like fun. I heard them make an announcement about Camp Timberlake in Sunday school last week. When I asked Dad about it, he said, "Let's plan on sending you next year. Okay?" By then I'll know the kids better so that's fine with me.

Did I tell you that the pastor came to visit us a couple of weeks ago? We didn't know he was coming, but Mom

59

had just baked some cookies so we ate them and just sat around getting to know each other. It was good to find out that a pastor can be just a regular guy. He didn't preach or anything but we did talk about God some. Then, before he left he asked Dad if he could pray with us. He said a short prayer–not the long kind like he prays before the sermon every Sunday. I like the way he prays–even the long ones. It seems like he's just talking to God like he would talk to a friend.

Time to go! Write and tell me about camp!

Terry

August 24

Dear Terry,

Howdy! Boy did I have a great time at camp. Theresa and I were bunk-mates. She's lots of fun. She'll usually laugh at just about anything. She has her serious times too and she's a special friend. We spend lots of Sunday afternoons at each other's houses. When I go home from church with her I usually get to eat out at a restaurant with her family. At my house she just gets to share the roast beef, but she seems to like coming over and gets along good with my mom.

There were about two hundred girls at camp all week. NO BOYS! When you get that many girls together there's lots of fun and giggling. Boys would ruin it all. Mom says that someday I'll be anxious to have boys around but I really doubt it. In Jr. High Camp and High School Camp, the boys and girls go to camp the same week. There's a hill of boys' cabins and a hill of girls' cabins. The older girls at my church seem to think it's a big deal to have a boy invite you to sit with him at the banquet on the last night of camp.

At camp we swam a lot, played softball, dodge ball, made crafts, ate gross food, and spent a lot of money on candy and stuff from the canteen! We sang lots of funny, goofy songs in the dining hall.

My counselor was really nice. She's working at camp for the whole summer. I think I'd like to do that when I'm older.

School starts soon. Can you believe we'll be in sixth grade? I've been asking Mary, my sister, what sixth grade is like. She says we'll be working on creative writing, diagraming sentences, studying the solar system, and coloring lots of maps. She hated it but she always says that about school. I don't think it will be too bad.

Tomorrow we're going out to buy school supplies. That's always one of my favorite things to do because we really splurge and eat out somewhere. Going out for hamburgers and French fries only happens twice a year in our family—once for school shopping and once when Mom and Dad get their income tax refund check.

I REALLY liked the poem you sent. Could you send some more? I'm not very good at writing poems. You should have an easy time with Creative Writing class!

Well, I better get my chores done early today before Dad comes home from work. Write soon and tell me about sixth grade. When does your school start?

Love,

Joyce

August 25

Dear Joyce,

I've got important news. I got saved this Sunday!! That's right–I asked Jesus to come into my heart and I know He did. Here's how it happened.

Of course you know I've been thinking a lot and learning more about God. I really wanted to understand how to give my life to Him like you and like my mom. So Sunday I really listened to Pastor Egner. It seemed like he was talking right to me when he preached. He talked about us needing to admit we are sinners and I started feeling like something was eating at my insides.

All I could think about were the times I had lied and been mad at my dad and mom. And there was a time when I was six years old when I went to a friend's birthday party with lots of other kids. We were playing games and each game had a winner. The prizes they were winning were fun ones but I didn't win anything. I'm ashamed to tell you that I stole someone's yo-yo and hid it in my pocket. I remember thinking I would have so much fun with it but then I couldn't even stand to look at it. Later when I decided to tell Mom what I had done I found out she already knew. The boy's mother had called to see if I'd brought it home by mistake. Mom had just been waiting to see if I would confess.

Anyway, that morning in church as I thought about my life, I knew I was a sinner. Maybe I was usually a good, honest kid, but compared to a perfect and holy God I felt filthy and rotten. Pastor Egner said God couldn't let even one sin into heaven. So if we want to go to heaven something must be done about our sins. Now I could understand it clearly. That's why Jesus came to die on the cross. He suffered so I wouldn't have to suffer and pay for my sins forever in hell.

I couldn't wait till they started singing the last hymn. I walked to the front and my Sunday school teacher explained some more and prayed with me as I asked Jesus to be my Saviour. It was the first time in my life that I had ever talked to God!

I've even memorized two Bible verses this week. Here's I John 5:11-12—

"And this is the record, that God hath given to us eternal life, and this life is in his Son. He that hath the Son hath life; and he that hath not the Son of God hath not life."

I'm working on verse thirteen too. I didn't see it happen, but after I went forward, Dad walked up to the front. He told Pastor Egner that he was ready to live for Jesus. GREAT!! Now our whole family is saved!! Dad and I are getting baptized soon. Wish you could see my happy face on that day. It just makes me want to shout and tell the whole world how good God is!

I think I'll love going to camp next summer. Hope I go for sure. Sounds like you had a blast!

Why do you hate boys so much? Are they really that bad? I don't see why a boy and a girl can't be friends. I don't mean boyfriend and girlfriend or any of that mushy stuff people are always teasing about. But can't they just like some of the same things and enjoy playing together sometimes? I think they can. Please write and tell me what you think.

In Jesus,

Terry

P.S. I can't wait for school to start again. I just know music and choir will be my favorite classes–art too!

August 30

Dear Terry,

I'm soooooooooo excited to hear that you accepted Christ! And you know what? You're not an only (lonely) child anymore. I'm your sister in God's family. In fact, we both have tons of sisters and brothers in Christ. Of course that doesn't mean we'll live at the same address or anything like that but you CAN know that you're never alone. Jesus promises to never leave His children. Isn't that great?

I can't write any more tonight but I had to tell you how happy I am for you–and for your dad too!!

Your Sister in Christ,

Joyce

October 2

Dear Terry,

I'm sorry that I haven't written in over a month. I've been busy with homework and everything seems harder because I'm so worried about Granny. She's not doing well at all. She doesn't even recognize my aunts–the ones who take care of her. She calls them "THAT WOMAN" and things like that. She sleeps most of the time I guess and they even have to help her eat. I know I won't get another birthday letter from her. But I got out her letters from other years and read them. That helped. I wish you could have met Granny before she got sick. Here's one of my favorite birthday letters from her:

Dear Joyce,

Tomorrow you'll turn seven, God's perfect number. Of course no one is perfect and I don't expect you to be either. Never forget, though, that God loves you perfectly and His perfect love can cast away all your fears (I John 4:18).

You've made me so proud over the years and I know you will continue to be a sweet girl who loves the Lord and wants to please Him. I prayed for you every day of your sixth year. And I'll pray for you each day of this coming year that God will keep you safe and in His perfect will.

I'm sending along seven silver dollars–one for each year of joy you've brought to me and to your family. Always remember that I love you dearly and I always will.

A bundle of love,
Granny

Oh, how I wish God would let me have Granny back the way she was!

It's good to be able to tell you about Granny. What else can I write about? Let's see. Our Sunday school class is having a contest to see who can bring the most visitors. It's a good way to bring more people to church so they can hear about Jesus. I'm working hard to win. In our other church a boy beat me two years in a row and I don't want to lose to a BOY again this year! Even if you do think boys and girls can be friends, I like to beat them whenever I can! (I guess you're probably right about being friends, though.)

I agree with you about music class being a favorite. It's my favorite time of the week. My whole family likes to sing together in the car. I want to learn to sing harmony like my mom.

Last week Dad brought home three five-gallon metal barrels. I don't know what used to be in them but he got them for free. They are very sturdy and we've been having a blast with them after school every day. I've learned to walk on them backwards and forwards for quite a ways without falling off. I even beat Donna in a race. The neighbors have all been over trying to learn how too. It seems like that's all we do after school every day now. If we get tired of walking on them, we start jumping over them like hurdles. We keep moving two of them farther and farther apart to see who can jump over them without stepping in between.

Do you have much homework this year? It sure isn't fun to bring schoolwork home all the time.

Yesterday after dinner we girls had a family auction. I guess you wouldn't know what that is. Well, we made it up last summer when we were bored. We each get out some things we want to trade with each other and start offering what we will trade and what we want in return. (Sometimes we call them trading parties.) I've gotten some of my favorite toys that way! Last night I traded a little coin purse to Kathy for a ball and jacks. Do you like to play jacks? Kathy thinks she is too old for that now.

Write when you have time.

God Bless You!

Joyce

P.S. Will you send more of your poems sometime? You're good at them!

October 10

Dear Joyce,

Hi! How do you like sixth grade? Seems like it will be lots harder but no one has ever died from too much school work. At least that's what my mom says but I wonder if she's 100% sure about that!!

Mom hasn't been feeling well again. It sure is hard to see her sick so often. She keeps telling Dad and me that she feels fine but we can both see the pain in her eyes. I wish the doctors could figure out what's wrong with her. Dad and I have been doing the cooking and cleaning again. It makes me feel a little better to be helping out.

I can't help wondering if something serious is wrong and if Mom is going to die. I never tell anyone else that I think about death but it worries me sometimes–especially at night when I'm in bed. I guess you know what that fear is like because of your Granny. At least now I know what would happen if Mom died. She'd go to heaven and I'd see her again some day. But I guess I'm selfish because I'd rather keep her here with Dad and me. Is that how you feel? I think your Granny would want you to trust God for everything. It's hard, but I'm trying. Let's help each other in our letters if we can.

I'm sending a few more poems I wrote–hope your birthday's special. Gotta stop for now and do my homework. (YUK!)

Friends in Christ,

Terry

WHO DOES GOD WANT?

God wants you!
God wants me!
To be what we
ought to be.

To do for Him
What He does for me.
Don't you see?
God wants me!

WHO GOD LOVES

God loves everybody
Short or tall.
God loves everybody
Big or small.

God loves everybody
Bright or dull.
God loves everybody
One and all!

October 17

Dear Terry,

I <u>did</u> have a happy birthday, but my big news is–I won the Sunday school contest! I'm so excited! I got the most points for bringing visitors and extra points for finishing my Sunday school workbook every week. The prize was a tape recorder. Imagine that!! A tape recorder of my very own! It even has a microphone. My sisters and I talked on it and sang some songs today just to test it out. My voice sounded so funny on tape–not like I thought it should. I wonder if that's the way I always sound to other people?

Mary and I came up with a good idea of a joke to pull on Donna and Kathy one of these days. In fact we may try it out this Saturday when our cousins come to visit. We'll try to sneak into the room they're playing in and turn the tape recorder on. Then after about fifteen minutes we'll rewind it and play it back for them to hear. Theresa (my friend with the horse) said she taped two of her brothers once when they didn't know the recorder was on. She said it was really funny and even her brothers started laughing and forgot to be mad at her.

Today in Social Studies class our teacher told us we have to write a report about a state we would like to visit. Guess which state I'm choosing to write about? VERMONT!! I think it would be neat if you could send some pictures or maybe one of those travel brochures. No–I have a better idea. I'll send you some money and have you buy me some post cards of famous places in Vermont. Would that be okay? I could tape them to paper and then tell about each post card. What do you think? Do you have any ideas for a title?

Thanks for remembering my Granny, even when your mom is sick. I want to be more like you that way. And yes–let's help each other trust God more. That will really make us friends. Here's a verse for you–"Be of good courage, and he shall strengthen your heart, all ye that hope in the Lord" (Psalm 31:24).

Love,

Joyce

P.S. I liked your poems even better than the first one. Keep them coming!

October 28

Dear Joyce,

I'm sending your post cards with this letter. As you can see, Vermont is a beautiful state. Sometimes it's called the Green Mountain State because of the mountains that run through it.

How's the food in your school's cafeteria? Ours is absolutely, positively awful! Half the time you can look at it and still not know what it is. Even tasting it doesn't always give you a clue. School food never looks or tastes anything like Mom's or Dad's cooking but it makes less work for Mom if she doesn't have to worry about baking stuff for my lunch so I try to eat it. The only thing they make that is good is the pizza. YUM! It's the greatest.

On Wednesdays they have a sandwich-type thing that they call "mystery meat." Some of the kids joke about it being horse meat or dog meat but I'm sure it isn't. (It better not be!) On Fridays they always serve fish.

How many days will you have off for spring vacation? We have a whole two weeks. Our family may drive to Illinois to see Dad's relatives IF Mom is feeling well. That's a long way off though. It's not even November and I'm already anxious for Easter. Guess what?!! Mom asked me the other day if I'd like to stop in Iowa to see you. She said maybe we could stay in a motel in Cedar Rapids one night and make plans to meet you and your parents at a restaurant for dinner.

What do you think? Sounds like fun but I have to warn you not to get your hopes up. Mom's health is not dependable. Why don't you ask your folks and tell me what they say. Okay?

Your Friend,

Terry

November 5

Dear Terry,

Wow! YES! I would love to have you stop in Iowa this spring. I'm dying to meet you! Do you realize you have never sent me a picture of yourself? I've seen pictures of Muffy, Blondie . . . even a picture of your dad holding your huge bass . . . but I've never seen what YOU look like. Will you please send me a school picture this year or at least a snapshot? I promise I won't laugh at your freckles, use it as a dart board, or use it to scare mice away! Ha ha. You could be the ugliest girl on earth and I'd still like you. We have a very special friendship. TRUST ME! I will like you no matter what. Even if you look like Frankenstein (whoops– he's a boy, I think) we'd still be friends. I hope you believe me, because I mean what I say!!

Last week I spent some of my money and bought an autograph book. I've been taking it to school and church to have my friends sign it. Have you ever had one? This is my first one but it's fun. The pages are all different colors. I've been letting people choose which of my colored pens they want to write with. I'll copy some of my favorites from all the pages people have signed.

IF YOU LOVED ME LIKE I LOVE YOU–
WOULDN'T THAT BE FINE?
THEN I'D HAVE YOU AND YOU'D HAVE ME–
FOR A VALENTINE!

(Mrs. Steward–Sunday school teacher)

FRIENDS ARE LIKE DIAMONDS–
PRECIOUS AND RARE.
ENEMIES ARE LIKE AUTUMN LEAVES–
FOUND EVERYWHERE.
PLEASE MAKE ME A LINK IN YOUR GOLDEN
BRACELET OF FRIENDSHIP.

I love you,
Grandma Long

U R
2 GOOD
+ 2 BE
4 GOTTEN

Love–Trixie

Theresa
By writing UPSIDE DOWN!
Remember the girl who spoiled your book
Remember the girl in the town!
Remember the girl in the city!

My Dear Joyce,

Always live close to Jesus. He loves you and so do I. Have a very good school year.

My Love,
Aunt Jill

EAST-WEST
YOU'RE THE BEST!
From–Linda

Why can't a hand be more than eleven inches long?
Because if it was it would be a foot!

> Your Cousin,
> Dianne

Dear Joyce,
I like having you in my class this year. May you
always seek God's will in all that you do.

> *Love,*
> *Mrs. Howard*

Lots of people just signed their names, but I like it when
they write more, especially little poems or jokes to figure
out. When we see each other this spring I want you to sign
it–okay? I'm afraid to send it in the mail because if it got
lost I'd lose all those autographs and have to start over again.

> Love,

Joyce

November 30

Dear Joyce,

Hi! I liked reading about your autograph book. No—I've never had one of my own. In fact, I've never even signed one before. I'd be honored to sign yours if we see each other this spring. Maybe I could make up a special poem just for you. I'll try!

Someday I'll send you a picture of myself but I'm not sure when. That's all I want to say about it for right now! I won't forget, and I'll explain later.

What did you do for Thanksgiving? We went to visit my grandparents (the ones who live here in town). Three of my cousins were there. They're quite a bit younger than me (6–4–and 2) but it was still fun.

Mom's been feeling good this week. I could tell she enjoyed Thanksgiving dinner. This year I thought about all I have to be thankful for. It's the first Thanksgiving that I've ever talked to God and thanked Him for all He's done for me and my family.

Guess what? The doctor thinks Mom's sick headaches are migraines and he gave her a new medicine to try. If it doesn't help they may do a bunch of allergy tests but it seems to be helping a little. That's an answer to a lot of prayers. How's your Granny doing? Any better?

Gotta Go,

Terry

P.S. Christmas is only one month away!

December 10

Dear Terry,

Thanks for caring enough to ask about Granny. We used to be so close and now she can't even write me a letter–she doesn't even know who I am! I'm so thankful that God has helped me to trust Him to do what is best. Now, instead of being afraid she'll die, I'm ready for her to go to heaven. In heaven her mind and body will be well again!

I'm glad to hear your mom is feeling better. Tell her "hello" for me. I'm writing this letter from school. We had to stay in for recess because it's snowing and bitter cold out. When recess is canceled we get to play table games in the classrooms, color pictures, or just talk with friends. I decided to write a letter to tell you my idea for Mom and Dad's Christmas present. I know they'll love it but it won't cost me anything–at least not any money–just a lot of work.

I plan to give them a jar full of coupons. Each coupon will have something written on it that I'll do for them whenever they ask–no expiration date and no grumbling from me. What do you think? I'll cut them out and write on them with my best handwriting. Wish I was allowed to use Mom's typewriter. Then they'd look more official but then I guess it might take me a long time to type them since I don't know how. I'm gonna put them in a pretty jar I've been saving.

I've already made a list of what the coupons will say and how many of each one I will give. Here's my plan:

4—Dry Dishes
4—Wash Dishes
2—Take Out Garbage
4—Set Table
2—Fold Laundry
2—Go to Grandma's (so they can be alone)
2—Breakfast in Bed
3—Wash Car
4—Dust Furniture
3—Wild Card (good for anything you choose)
1—Clean Basement
1—Clean Garage

Well that's my idea. Do you like it? I wouldn't mind if you want to do it too.

I have no idea what to get my sisters and Keith. I only have $4.36. Maybe I could make coupons for them too. I'm not sure they'd like it though. Got any ideas?

Love,

Joyce

December 29

Dear Joyce,

We had a great Christmas! Even though there weren't as many gifts as usual because of all the doctor bills we need to pay, it was the best Christmas I've ever had. I always knew Christmas was Jesus' birthday but I never knew Jesus as my Saviour. That's made a big difference in our home this year.

We all talked about ways we could give Jesus a gift by giving to others in need. Each of us prayed about how much of our money we'd like to give. Then we gave the money to a special Christmas love offering at church. I got some nice gifts too, but best of all was knowing that Mom and Dad and I are all in God's family.

Two of Dad's brothers were visiting Grandma and Grandpa for Christmas. Dad comes from a family of six boys. Can you imagine that? My grandparents wanted a girl so bad but they never did get one–not until their sons started getting married–then they soon had six daughters-in-law.

I wrote this poem on Christmas Eve. I was thinking about how there are still so many people I know who haven't trusted Christ as their Saviour. I know God expects me to be a witness to them but sometimes that's scary. I'm so glad you weren't afraid to start writing to me about Jesus.

HARVEST

Is the harvest done?
No! It's only begun!
It won't be done
Until everyone's won
Then the harvest's done.

Friends in Christ,

Terry

P.S. Sure am looking forward to spring vacation–and our trip.

December 30

Terry,

I realized today that I've never told you much about my little brother Keith. He has freckles all over his nose. Whenever Mom or Dad used to take pictures of him he would squint or crinkle up his nose. Now when he sees those old pictures of himself he asks, ''What was the matter with my nose?'' I'm glad Keith came along or I'd still be the baby of the family. People say that Keith and I look like Dad.

This past Christmas was heartbreaking. After we had all opened our presents, my dad gathered up the box of wrappings and trash to burn while Mom cooked scrambled eggs. Keith was busy playing with one of his gifts–a red fire truck. Ten minutes later he was crying and screaming. At first we thought he was hurt, but finally he calmed down enough to tell us the problem. All of his other gifts were gone.

We all helped search the house. We looked everywhere– under the couch–in his room–but we finally figured out that Dad must have burned them with the trash by mistake. Keith hadn't been careful about separating the gifts from the ripped-up wrappings.

All of us were heartsick. No one felt as guilty as Dad though. He promised Keith they would be the first customers at the store to buy new toys. This made Keith feel a little better but it was hard for him to stop sobbing. Later, when I was alone, I cried too. I knew Mom and Dad couldn't afford to replace those presents.

Just before supper that night, Kathy whispered to Donna and Mary and me to come into our bedroom. "I've got an idea," she said. "Keith sure liked that little flashlight I got, so I'm going to give it to him. Then Mom and Dad won't have to buy so many new presents."

That made the rest of us decide to do the same thing. I gave Keith a box of felt-tip pens I'd gotten, and Mary gave him a cute little wooden dog that comes apart into puzzle pieces. None of Donna's presents seemed right for Keith (he's not crazy about horses like she is) so she's going to get Dad to return her new horse book and buy Keith a book he'd really like. He's going to end up with plenty of presents!

Then I started thinking about how God gives us things. Our family doesn't have much money to spare after the bills are all paid but God always gives us what we really need. I'm not sure how Mom and Dad are managing to pay for the braces I have to get next year but the dentist said I need them badly so they'll find a way. It makes me feel guilty and yet special too. I'm learning that there are lots of things more important than money.

Your Friend,

Joyce

February 21

Dear Terry,

You've probably been as busy as I have these past few weeks, but I wanted to send you this picture of our whole family. It was taken for the church directory but each family was allowed to order extra copies. Mom bought lots of them to send in Christmas cards but she still had some left so she gave each of us two pictures. I kept one for my scrapbook and decided to give you one. You can tell I've changed since the last school picture I sent to you in fifth grade. I always hate seeing pictures of myself. My mom always seems to cut my bangs crooked so I look strange.

My sister Kathy made all the look-alike dresses for Mother's Day last spring. She's a great seamstress and doesn't mind all the work. We girls don't always feel like wearing the dresses when Mom tells us to. The good part is that at least once in a while I get a NEW dress that no one else has worn and passed down! It's a nice change.

Talking about Mother's Day reminds me of a story about my mom when she was a young girl. Mom was the youngest of seven children. She was ten or eleven when her two older brothers graduated and joined the army. Granny had to work after her husband died and most of Mom's older sisters worked too. Mom was home alone after school most of the time and she hated it. One of the things she used to do to fill the time was write letters to her brothers in the army. One year around Mother's Day when Mom was about eleven or twelve, she bought each of her brothers a Mother's Day card and sent it along with best wishes and a letter. Of course, her brothers were the laughingstock of their barracks when the other soldiers saw they had gotten Mother's Day cards! It was really funny but what made it even funnier was that Mom wasn't trying to make a joke. She had never stopped to realize that people only gave cards to MOTHERS on Mother's Day. Her family teased her about that for a long time!

I like to hear stories about funny things us kids did when we were little. Mom tells one story about a time when I was four years old. I had caught a cold and one morning after breakfast my mom said, "Why Joyce–you're a little hoarse today." Almost in tears I answered her, "No Mommy! I not a little horse. I a little lady!"

Bye for now!

Joyce

P.S. There's nothing new about Granny. I'm still trusting the Lord for her. How's your mom doing?
P.P.S. Just think! In about six weeks you might be here! I can hardly wait.

March 20

Dear Joyce,

In two weeks we'll see each other. In two days (or maybe three) you'll get an envelope from me with my picture inside but no letter. I'm not sending it with this letter because I want to explain something before you see what I look like.

There's something about me that you don't know because I've never told you. Remember when I told you I was almost sure I'd never go to a mother-daughter banquet? I told you that someday you'd know why. Well, today is the day.

You've asked many times for a picture of me but I've never sent one. I've also never signed my letters "SISTERS in Christ." When I've talked about my friends, I've never told you their names. Is it starting to make sense?

What I have to say is very hard but I guess I just need to come right out and tell you. Remember when I asked you why you hate boys and I tried to change your mind? Well, I had a good reason for it. My name is not short for Theresa like your friend from church. It's short for Terrance. I'm a boy!

Please don't get mad and rip up this letter. Let me try to explain. When I sent my name in to the magazine where your Granny found it, I just signed my name, "Terry." That's what everyone calls me. Hardly anyone knows my real name. I wasn't even thinking someone might think I was a GIRL wanting a pen pal.

DEAR TERRY

When I got your first letter, of course I realized you were a girl. I didn't know what to do. I'd been waiting six months for a pen pal but I wanted a boy. I decided it would be fun to write to you a few more times and then surprise you with the news. But the more I read your letters, the more I wanted to be friends so I kept putting off telling you. I thought if I waited long enough you'd want to keep being friends anyway. I hope that is what you'll do now.

We've been writing a long time and you're my best friend. I don't care if you are a girl. I hope you'll still want to write and keep on being pen pals. If it hadn't been for you and your letters and prayers I may never have become a Christian.

If you don't want to meet me, please write and tell me. I will understand even though I hope that won't happen.

Still Friends??